PUFFIN BOOKS

Wry Rhymes
for Troublesome Times

Irrepressible fun from a master of the absurd poem. This delightful collection of light-hearted verse takes a refreshing sideways look at the world and all that there is in it, including: orbiting aunts, forgetful fathers, bike-freak brothers, sandal thongs, snails, wings and things and briny bits.

A collection to attract, intrigue, amuse and surprise, with hilarious illustrations by Michael Atchison.

A superb follow-up to *Songs for My Dog and Other People*, also published in Puffin.

Also by Max Fatchen
Songs for My Dog and Other People

Max Fatchen
Wry Rhymes
for Troublesome Times

illustrated by Michael Atchison

PUFFIN BOOKS

PUFFIN BOOKS

Published by the Penguin Group
27 Wrights Lane, London W8 5TZ, England
Viking Penguin Inc., 40 West 23rd Street, New York, New York 10010, USA
Penguin Books Australia Ltd, Ringwood, Victoria, Australia
Penguin Books Canada Ltd, 2801 John Street, Markham, Ontario, Canada L3R 1B4
Penguin Books (NZ) Ltd, 182–190 Wairau Road, Auckland 10, New Zealand

Penguin Books Ltd, Registered Offices: Harmondsworth, Middlesex, England

First published by Kestrel Books 1983
Published in Puffin Books 1985
10 9 8 7 6 5

Made and printed in Great Britain by
Richard Clay Ltd, Bungay, Suffolk
Filmset in Monophoto Baskerville

For Jean and Olga

Contents

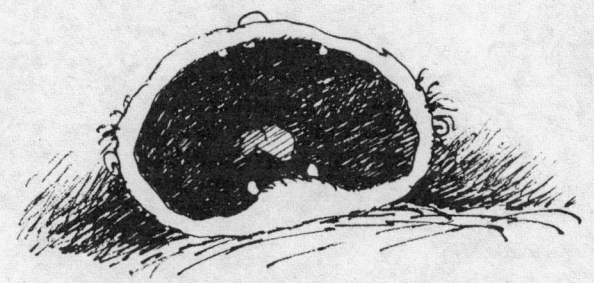

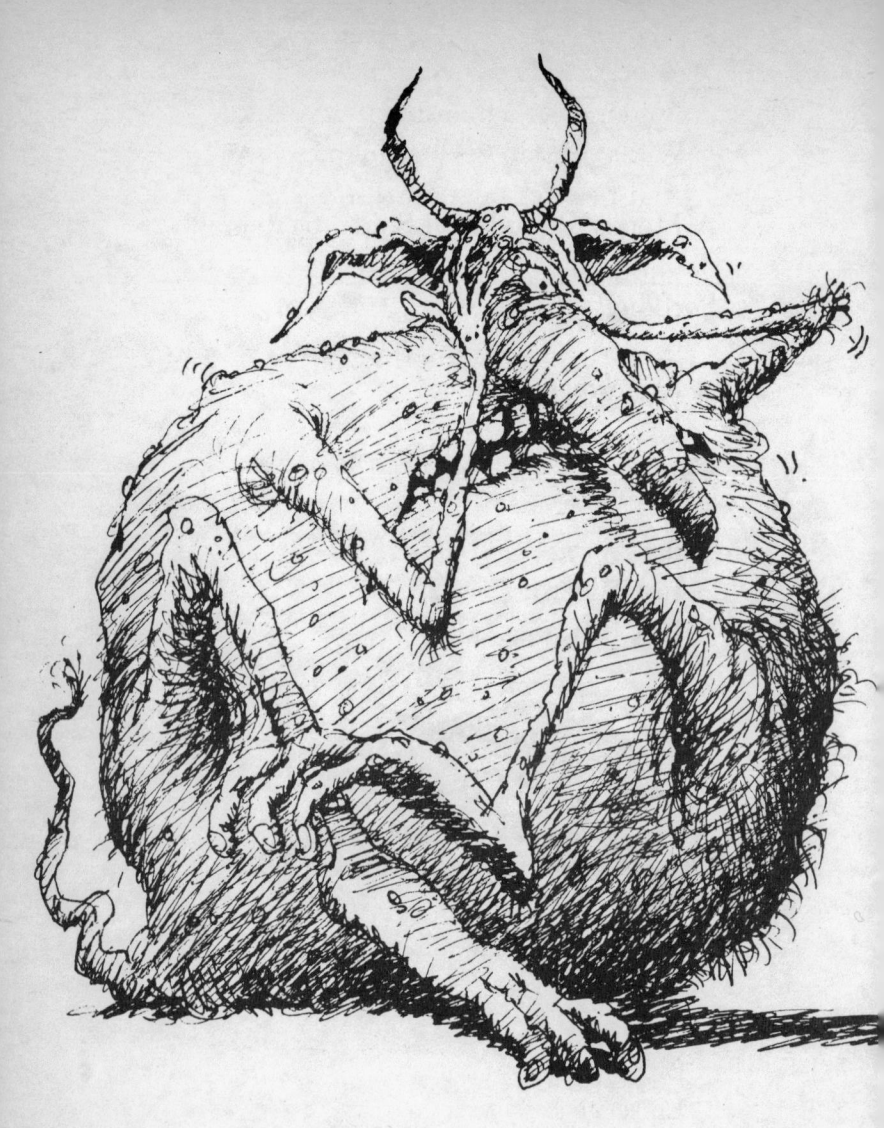

I often meet a monster
While deep in sleep at night;
And I confess to some distress.
It gives me quite a fright.
But then again I wonder.
I have this thought, you see.
Do little sleeping monsters scream
Who dream
Of meeting me?

Windowsills and Railway Thrills

WINDOWSILLS

A windowsill seems a nice spot to sit
For a box of bright flowers or a sparrow,
But for children who want to relax for a bit
They make them a little too narrow.

You can lean on a windowsill, looking outside,
With your hands propping under your chin
To a world that is rolling, both restless and wide
From the warm little world that you're in.

The windowsill gathers the dust, but again
There's someone who's keeping it clean.
You can coat it with varnish (so people explain)
Or paint it a pot-planty green.

I think that the man who invented them said,
'The sill of the window? Oh that.
It's a simple idea that I had in my head
As a place for my sun-loving cat.'

ORBIT AN AUNT

Some day
I wish that Aunty May
Could join the race
As the first aunt
Into Space.
It would save her peering
And interfering,
Lifting saucepan lids
And chastising kids.

Then, instead,
I could point overhead,
'LOOK!...
Just left of the Milky Way,
That's Aunty May.'

THE RAILWAY HISTORICAL
STEAM WEEKEND

'Will you come,' says the letter, 'and join our
    outing.
Meal provided and time to spend
Along a line that is rarely travelled
For the railway historical steam weekend.'

The guard is dressed in his railway splendour,
With buttons and braid in a beautiful blend.
The engine's green, with a shining tender
For the railway historical steam weekend.

We stare at the signals old and ailing,
Our carriages labelled with their class.
The luggage rack has a real brass railing
And larks awake in the railyard grass.

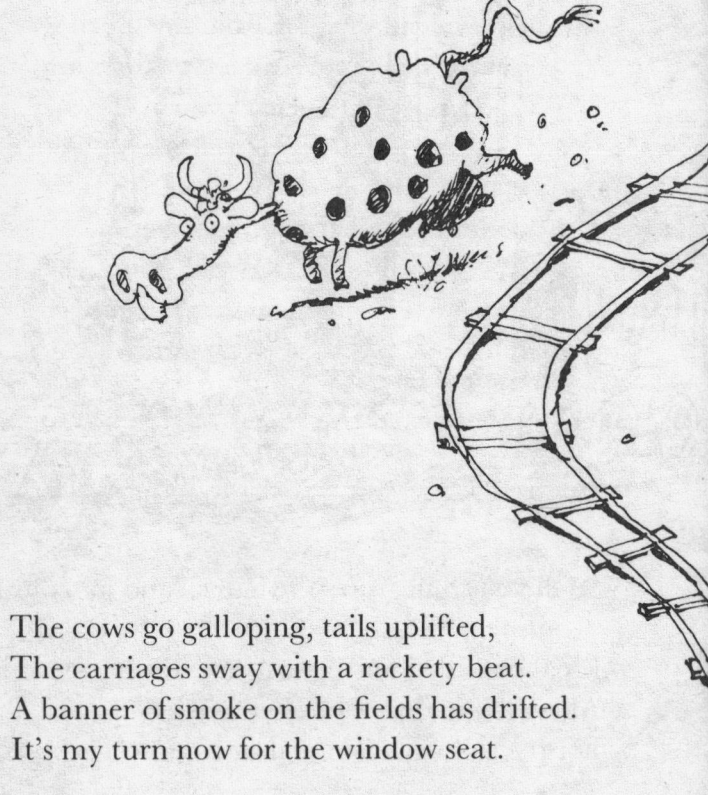

The cows go galloping, tails uplifted,
The carriages sway with a rackety beat.
A banner of smoke on the fields has drifted.
It's my turn now for the window seat.

There's a leather smell from the green seat covers.
The woodwork moves in a creaking song,
With corridors full of railway lovers
All pushing about where they don't belong.

My father's loaded with information
On regulations and rules and Acts
And pages and pages on varying gauges
And funnels and tunnels and railway facts.

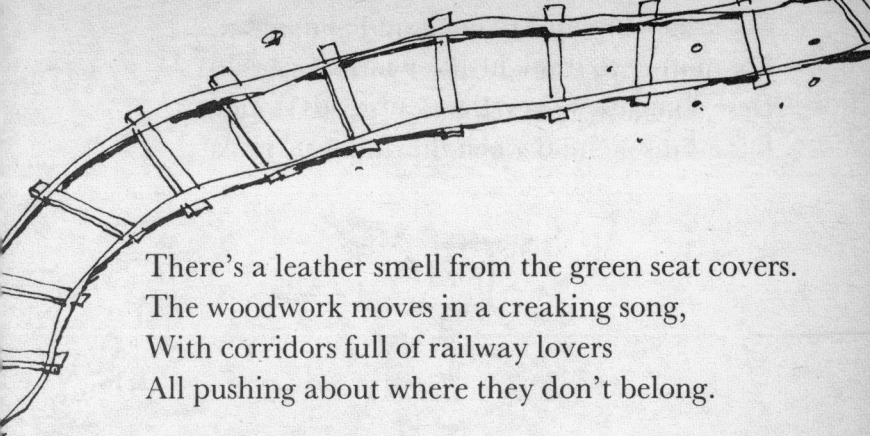

My father explains that it's quite improper
For mother to think he has wheels for brains
Describing expresses, the slow goods stopper,
But adults go mad when they play at trains.

So he looks at his watch as our time grows shorter,
Announcing the stations along our run.
He's wearing a cap with the title 'Porter'
For he likes to join in the railway fun.

We huff through cuttings with old rockfaces
And clatter on bridges above slow creeks
To all the mysterious railway places,
With a coal-black smudge on our wind-whipped
   cheeks.

We visit the engine at one small siding,
It hisses and pants like an iron god.
The driver is peering and prodding at pistons
And poking the great connecting rod.

Then on again with the white steam spouting
While signals dip near the journey's end.
My father says what a splendid outing,
A most educational steam weekend . . .

Well-organized and a worthwhile function,
With smoky wind and the rocking bend.
(But I liked tea at the local junction
On the railway historical steam weekend.)

Ruinous Rhymes

Pussycat, pussycat, where have you been,
Licking your lips with your whiskers so clean?
Pussycat, pussycat, purring and pudgy,
Pussycat, pussycat. WHERE IS OUR BUDGIE?

This little pig went to market
But I think that the point is well taken –
It's the cute little pig that wisely stayed home
Who succeeded in saving his bacon.

Mary, Mary, quite contrary,
How does your garden grow?
With snails and frogs and neighbours' dogs
And terribly, terribly slow.

Sing a song of sixpence?
It's hardly worth the sound.
So if you want my singing
Please offer me a pound.

When Old Mother Hubbard
Went to the cupboard
Her dog for a morsel would beg.
'Not a scrap can be found,'
She explained to her hound
So he bit the poor dear on the leg.

Proceed With Care: Parents Ahead

'WE WON'T TELL YOU AGAIN!'

It makes me sullen and wilful and wild
The way I'm described as a difficult child.
They shake their heads wherever I go
And tell each other, 'I told you so.'
They tell each other and even a friend,
'We don't quite know where it all will end.'
And tale on tale they have mournfully piled
On the life they lead with a difficult child.

But when I'm sweet and I smile and purr,
They say to each other, 'Now what's with her?'
And when I'm cuddly and kind and warm,
They say it's the calm before the storm.
And when I offer a hug or kiss
They're murmuring, 'What are you up to, Miss?'

JUST FANCY THAT

'Just fancy that!' my parents say
At anything I mention.
They always seem so far away
And never pay attention.

'Just fancy that,' their eyes are glazed.
It grows so very wearing.
'Just fancy that' is not a line
For which I'm really caring.

And so today I'm telling them
I threw a cricket bat.
I broke a windowpane at school.
They murmur, 'Fancy that.'

I wrote a message on the fence.
I spoke a wicked word.
The way the vicar hurried past,
I'm positive he heard.

'Just fancy that.' Then suddenly
Their eyes are sticking out,
Their words are coming in a rush
Their voices in a shout.

'You naughty child, you shameless boy,
It's time WE had a chat.'
Hurrah, they've noticed me at last.
My goodness, fancy that!

SO FORGETFUL!

My father's memory is absolutely unique,
He can remember footballers, horses
And what won last week.
He knows about fishing bait,
The economy's state,
When to post his Pools
And what's wrong with schools.
His figures are never-ending
About Government spending;
But isn't it funny?
And I'll be perfectly frank,
When it comes to remembering my pocket-money,
His mind goes blank.

'Your room is like a pigsty,'
Say some in tones of doom;
But older pigs scold younger pigs,
'Your pigsty's like a room.'

A SHORT, SUMMERY THIN, THONG SONG

The song
of a
thong
is a
flip,
flap,
flong
that echoes
wherever
you go.
There aren't
any places
for silly
old laces
but a thing
that holds
on to
your toe.

You're flapping
and tapping
with feet
overlapping
and people who watch
will agree
that the song
of a thong
when you're
flopping along
is of feet
that are born
to be
free.

Crafty Creatures

The flea is small
And no one's pet
But likes to hear
Of Dogs to Let.

There's nothing new about the gnu
That I could tell you here.
When young gnus play,
Tired mothers say,
'Don't be a *gnu*isance, dear.'

A waiting tortoise, looking cross,
Was answered by his mate.
'I missed the bus
But why the fuss,
I'm only six months late.'

The ravenous snail
Makes a long, shining trail
While clad in the slimiest garb.
If it's feeling unwell
It retires to its shell
For a nap and a dose of bicarb.

Guinea-pigs proliferate
At a most alarming rate;
So you'd better heed a warning.
Have you counted them this morning?

BEWARE

This cunning creature in its lair,
You'll find, is lurking everywhere.
There may be one (or even two).
It could be sitting next to you.
With staring eyes it's on the prowl.
It gives a sudden roar (or howl)
And, in a flash, to your dismay
It's leaping forward to its prey.
Beware each night this fearful danger –
The dreaded telly channel changer.

Slow Down For Boys

OH, BROTHER!

My brother's a motorbike freak.
Each week,
He rides races
In the oddest places.
He climbs hills,
Has spills.
He speeds
And cruises.
He gets action,
Satisfaction,
But mostly,
He gets bruises.

CONTROL CALLING

Just when I am conducting
A manoeuvre tactical
On my spaceship galactical,
Using my unidentified-object locators,
With my forward disintegrators
Whamming and shooting,
And my astro-clad officers saluting
Amid the rocketry's swirls and swishes,
My sister Kate
Cries 'Activate'
And I'm back on earth,
Drying dishes.

'What ARE you doing, Rupert?'
There comes the same reply,
For Rupert answers, 'Nothing.'
And that's his daily cry.

'What are you DOING, Rupert?
Who broke the garden pot?'
But Rupert answers, 'Nothing.'
And nothing's not a lot.

Whenever people blame him
For doing such-and-such
Then Rupert's doing nothing,
Which isn't very much.

'We want to SEE you, Rupert,
Who made this awful mess?'
But Rupert's doing nothing.
Well, nothing more or less.

And so we have this problem
To puzzle anyone,
How Rupert's doing nothing,
Yet naughty things get done.

Little Jim at last is clean.
They put him in the wash-machine.
He spun and dried without a sound.
Now there's a boy who's been around.

RANDOM ROT

'Children should be seen not heard.'
May I add a weary word?
Baby Bruce whose teeth aren't right
Loud and clear, is heard all night.

If they can muffle motorcars
Then why not noiseless cookie-jars?

Wings and Things

DINNER IS SERVED

When our almonds are ripe in the wind-shaken trees
And I'm thinking of one I might choose,
Then in from the ranges, with screeching delight
Comes a party of white cockatoos.

I don't recall sending a dinner-time card
Or asking them into my tree,
Or dropping the poor little shells in my yard
In the midst of their cockatoo tea.

What, dressing for dinner? Well yes, in a way
They're dressed in their cockatoo best,
Their snowy white plumage they nicely display,
With a bright yellow tinge on their crest.

They sit on the branches and hold in their claws
The almonds I've hoarded for weeks;
And they eat them with pleasure and never a pause
With a crack of their business-like beaks.

Almond cake I had planned for a party one night,
Almond toffee of rich, golden hues,
Alas with my plans they have all taken flight
Inside of those white cockatoos.

A wonderful bird is the pelican,
His bill will hold more than his belican.

A pelican, who heard this verse,
Remarked to me, 'Good gracious,
I know my stomach and my bill
Are what you'd call capacious

'And yet a reputation that
For food and fish I scrimmage
Will mark me as a greedy bird
And somewhat spoil my image.

'I do admit, well now and then,
Inside my bill I'm popping
Unwary fish, but then again
It's handy too for shopping.

'And so before I leave I must
In case I'm thought neglectful
Explain it so you'll be, I trust,
A little more respectful.

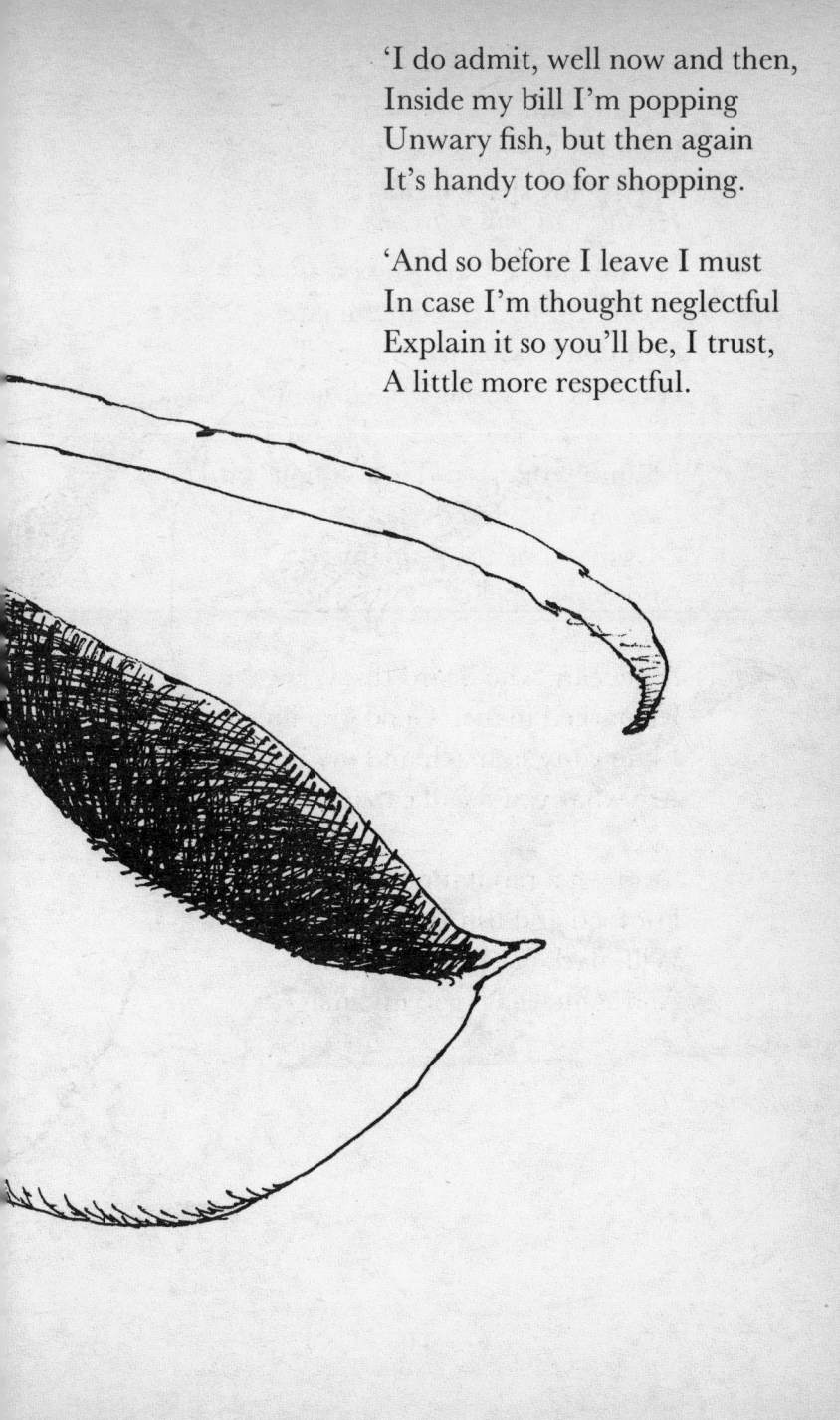

'The great advantage of a bill
Which cannot be denied,
Is simply opening it to fill
The roomy space inside.

'So any morsel, straying past,
Could finish in this catchment
And that is why my bill and I
Have such a strong attachment.'

I humbly thanked this pompous bird.
I've now a different slant
On what a pelican can do
And what a pelican't.

If pigs flew
And birds grunted
The world would seem
All back-to-fronted.

Poor Doris, so terribly tender
Was somehow caught up in a blender.
It beat her to pulp
And well you might gulp.
The chances are slim that they'll mend her.

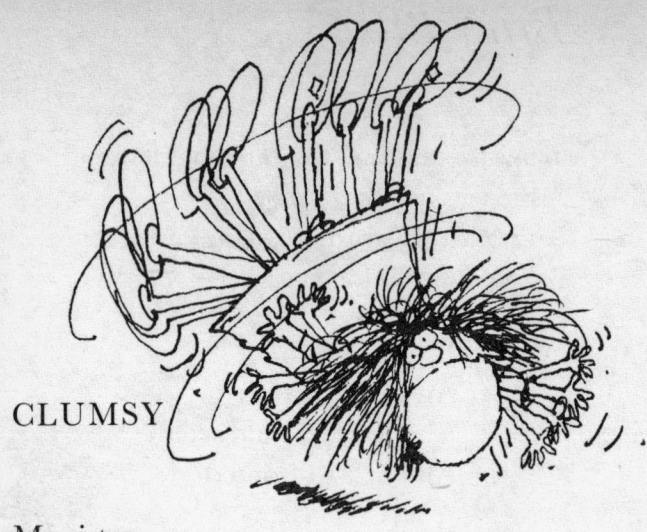

CLUMSY

My sister
 trips
  over any old thing
  while giving
   the loudest
   of squeals;
    over shoes,
     over mats,
      over chairs,
      over cats
       and finally
        head over heels.

Briny Bits

The boy stood on the burning deck,
A braver lad than most,
And said: 'It's rather warm for feet
But wonderful for toast.'

There occurred a most terrible scene
When a ship of the Merchant Marine
Lost a cargo of soap
At the Cape of Good Hope
And none of the crew would come clean.

Said a whale to her daughter whose spouting
Brought sailormen pointing and shouting,
'When they cry "Thar she blows"
Please attend to your nose
Or this is the end of your outing.'

Mermaids no longer croon the songs
That sailors found rewarding
For now they rock around the dock
And play a tape-recording.

ROWBOATS

I like rowboats, little rowboats,
Where you dip the oars and glide,
Listening to the seagull chatter
And the talking of the tide.

Sister Betty's at the tiller.
She has volunteered to steer.
Shep, the dog, is barking for'ard,
Keeping other vessels clear.

I'm the captain, giving orders,
Writing entries in the log,
Ready for repelling boarders,
Who will dare an old sea-dog?

Now we're Vikings from the Northland,
Taking longboats through the spray,
Writing in my longboat logbook,
'Sacked another town today.'

Was there ever such an ocean,
Spouting whales and Pirate Jack?
Sister Betty's suncream lotion
Oozes down her speckled back.

Gently on the wavelets pitching,
Listening to the sea's old sound,
Betty moans her nose is itching.
'LOOK OUT, BETTY! WE'RE AGROUND.'

Arms and legs and oars all flailing.
Words that make the paintwork blister.
When the seven seas you're sailing,
NEVER take a sunburnt sister!

Relax and Play, or Blow Away

IT'S A BIT RICH

Playing Monopoly's
Really my scene.
I hang on to houses
And play very mean.

I take all the money.
There's often a stack.
I'm not very pleasant
When giving it back.

I'm harsh as a landlord.
I've nothing for sale.
I'm buying your station.
You're going to jail.

My fistful of money –
It seems such a shame
When bedtime arrives
And it's only a game.

IT'S DONE THIS WAY

My father's twisting it about.
He says, 'I'll get the darn thing out.'
We try to help him if we can.
He says: 'This problem takes a man.'
His eyebrows knit. He sits, he stands,
This baffling object in his hands.
He twists, he frets, perspires and fumes
While we escape to other rooms.
Then finally, in deep despair,
He slumps defeated in his chair.
My father is an awful boob.
He's failed AGAIN with Rubik's Cube.

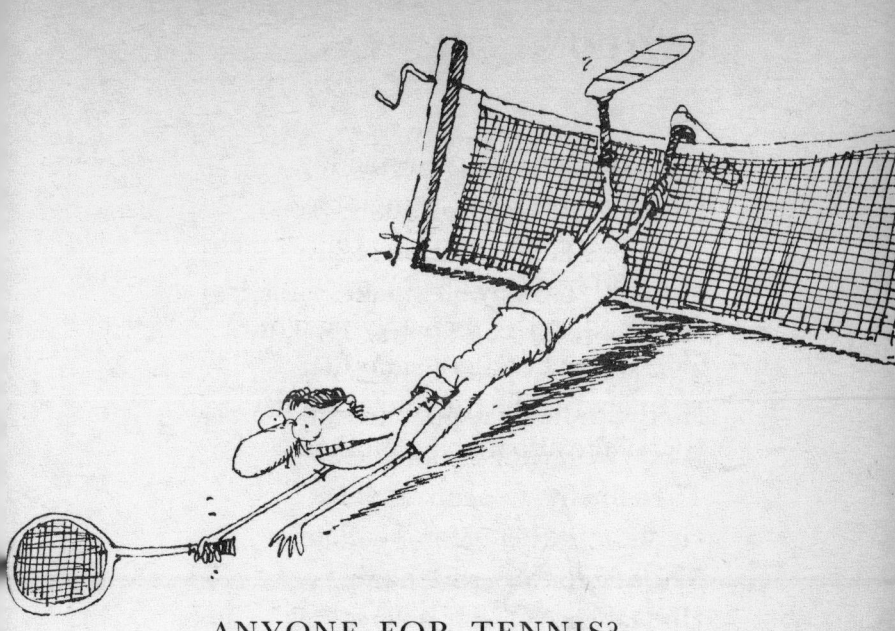

ANYONE FOR TENNIS?

When they shouted, 'Game and set,'
Cousin Henry jumped the net.
He came a thud upon his head
And now plays dominoes instead.

WINDY

The gale upon our holidays
Was not your passing breeze.
It gave our tents a fearful wrench
And bent the frantic trees.
So, if you've seen a flying tent,
And then observe another,
Please call us at your earliest,
We're also missing mother.

THEY'RE AWFUL

I hate them a lot . . .
People who are always telling the plot
Of television serials,
And how books end,
The menu for dinner,
Whether it's cold or hot;
Who always want to ride in the front seat of cars,
Whether it's their place
Or not
And who are always interrupting
And shouting,
'WHAT?'
I hate the lot.

SOMEWHERE

It's somewhere round the corner
Or so I've heard them say
And everybody wants to go
But no one knows the way.

The days are full of summer
And staying by the sea.
There's apple pie for breakfast
And what you like for tea.

And even running messages
Can be a lot of fun
While washing's not compulsory
And hair can stay undone.

Where chocolates are handy;
Please take another box.
Where only older people
Have mumps or chickenpox.

Where teachers are well hidden
And if you want the truth,
The dentist is forbidden
To touch another tooth.

The people spend their evenings
By walking on their hands
While motorcars are driven
By mostly rubber bands.

And there will be no shrieking
On what a child should do
With parents never speaking
Unless they're spoken to.

With never smell of cartridge
For guns are out of bounds.
Oh happy is the partridge
While foxes chase the hounds.

Where every tree is singing;
Where every bird is free.
With apple pie for breakfast
And what you like for tea.

No television cricket;
No giving up my chair.
I'd like to buy a ticket
If only I knew where.

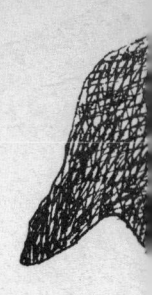

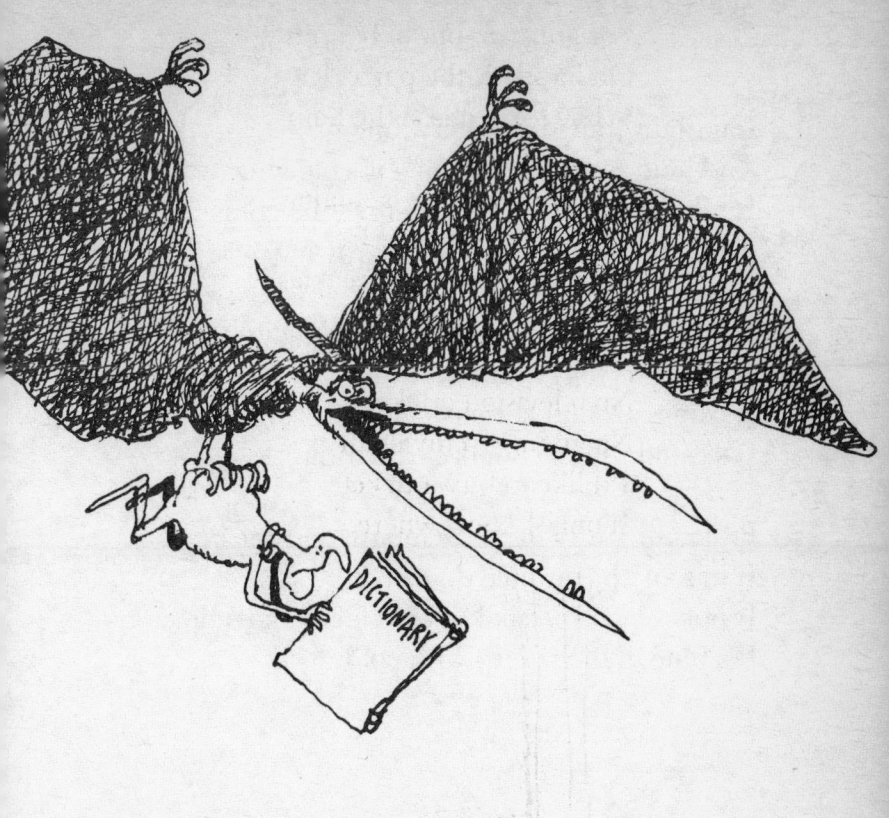

A moody pterodactyl said,
'I'm fearsome so they tell me.
Though grandly named, I'm so ashamed
That nobody can spell me.'

SO LONG!

Jonathan Jones has a very long nose
And loud is the sound when it's blowing.
It always precedes him wherever he goes
And somehow it seems to be growing.

Such a nose is a wonder but not a delight
And others may find it a strain.
It comes around corners before he's in sight.
It's caught in the doors of the train.

Protruding way over the mouth and the lip
It has an appearance that's bold.
It pokes into milkshakes with foam on its tip.
It's blue in the winter with cold.

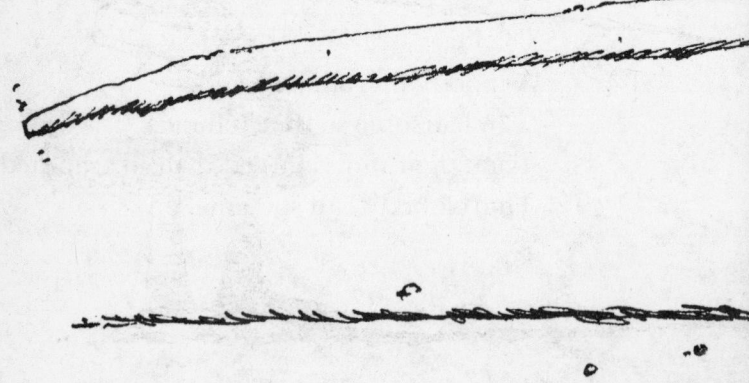

They've used it for hanging with washing and pots
With little success, I'm afraid.
It's sunburnt in summer with freckles and spots
Though children can sit in its shade.

It's a nuisance sometimes for Jonathan Jones
But the reason he never grows thinner
Is the way that his nose will inhale as it glows –
All the glorious smells of his dinner.

When father does the carving,
It's wiser not to linger.
With any luck he'll carve the duck
But, now and then, a finger.

Little Mary, looking wistful,
Eats her jelly by the fistful.
On the floor it slips and sloshes,
That's why everyone wears goloshes.

Young Arthur has an appetite
You simply can't ignore.
While other people have enough
He always asks for more.
He sets about his eating task
And leaves us so unnerved
One question that we NEVER ask
Is, 'Are you being served?'

COUNTRY LUNCH

The basket is a big one, the billycan immense.
We carry them so carefully when getting through the
    fence.
The wind is full of hay smell and hawks patrol the
    sky.
      When we take the lunches out,
      Jeremy and I.

The harvester is whirring, it cuts the heads of wheat,
The dusty whirlwinds spiralling in columns through
    the heat.
There could be summer snakes about, or so our
    mother said.
      That's why we're walking warily
      And watching where we tread.

We've seen the paddock growing, for magical the
    rain,
With each stalk putting out its flags and nourishing
    its grain.
We've seen old farmers shaking heads because the
    season's dry;
      And we have been a part of it,
      Jeremy and I.

For country folk are worriers and though it's not a
   crime,
Yet parents seem (says Jeremy) to do it all the
   time . . .
The bills, the taxes and the kids and how the dams
   are low
     And so it sets us wondering
     Why people worry so.

But then it happens. Storms arrive and creeks go
   mad and flood
And there is gold in every drop and diamonds in the
   mud.
The neighbours call to celebrate, with sausage-rolls
   and tea
     And everything comes right again
     For Jeremy and me.

So now we take the lunches out. It's 'Hurry up, you
   kids'.
Undoing of the luncheon wraps and rattling billy-
   lids,
With half a dozen messages. You'll need to
   understand.
     It's hurry, hurry, hurry,
With people on the land.

The grain trucks for the silo, the agent for the sheep,
'Now you remember, Jeremy. Your brain is half-
  asleep,
We'll get another drum of fuel. It won't do any
  harm.'
       It's orders, orders, orders
       When living on a farm.

'The steak and kidney pie is nice. Your mother's
  quite a cook.'
Our father's eyes are wandering with that slow
  farmer's look
That touches crop and heat-hazed land and plainly
  it will tell
       He cares for me and Jeremy
       And loves his earth as well.

We help him with the pannikins and clean the crusty
  plate.
The crop is ripe for harvesting. Tonight he's working
  late.
The summer's full of wonder (and steak and kidney
  pie)
       When we take the lunch things home
       Jeremy and I.

Just . . .

JUST WHEN . . .

It's always the same.
Just when you're playing a game;
Just when it's exciting
And interesting
With everyone racing
And chasing,
Just when you're having so much fun,
Somebody always wants something done!

JUST IN CASE...

When it's nearly my birthday
And so that people won't be upset
Or forget,
I always think it's kinder,
Just as a reminder,
To leave notes on plates,
Hinting at dates.

Most of Me

EARS

Have you thought to give three cheers
For the usefulness of ears?
Ears will often spring surprises
Coming in such different sizes.
Ears are crinkled, even folded.
Ears turn pink when you are scolded.
Ears can have the oddest habits
Standing rather straight on rabbits.
Ears are little tape-recorders
Catching all the family orders.
Words, according to your mother,
Go in one and out the other.
Each side of your head you'll find them.
Don't forget to wash behind them.
Precious little thanks they'll earn you
Hearing things that don't concern you.

ELBOWS

The elbow has a certain charm
By being halfway up your arm.
Without it you'd be less than able
But never leave it on the table.

LIPSERVICE

Our lips,
Are meant for hisses
And kisses,
Wisecracks
And quips
But mine are mostly
For fish and chips.

HULLO, INSIDE

Physical-education slides
Show us shots of our insides.
Every day I pat my skin,
'Thanks for keeping it all in.'

TAILPIECE

Tongues we use for talking.
Hands we clasp and link.
Feet are meant for walking.
Heads are where we think.
Toes are what we wiggle.
Knees are what we bend.
Then there's what we sit on
And that's about the end.